Acknowledgem

A BIG THANK YOU TO CORINNE

WHO LOVES HER ANIMALS BUT STILL FOUND TIME TO EDIT.

A BIG THANK YOU TO GRACE DURNFORD

FOR MAKING SURE THE BOOK LOOKED ITS BEST.

LAST BUT NOT LEAST MY GRAND DAUGHTER, SARAH

FOR HER ENTHUSIASAM AND ENCOURAGEMENT

A Note from the Author

Here are ten tales; each can be read when there is not much time

but reading takes your fancy.

Enjoy…....

Lily Clark March 2012

Thank you Saffy

I hope you enjoy
my book.

Lily Clark.

CONTENTS

LilyPad Tales

Lily Clark

1

SPRING

"Nan, here"

"Ok just a minute."

"No Nan, NOW!" "What?" I ask, almost irritated by being disturbed, "what is it you want?"

"Look at this Nan" he says with excitement in his voice. Bending down, I try to see what it is my grandson wants to show me but try as I might I cannot see what I am supposed to be looking at.

"Where" I say

"There Nan, there" he says, pointing his finger at the small flower that has poked its head just above the earth. "Oh that, that's a crocus, one of the first flowers of spring; it's telling us that summer is almost here and that soon the weather will be warm, making even more flowers pop their heads out to say hallo." Getting up, I made my way back to the house, back to facing all the things I had planned to do that day.

Standing at the sink with my hands in my rubber gloves marked marigold, I begin to wonder how long has it been since I saw a marigold, even though they grow in my garden. Soon my memory takes me back to the time when, not long after moving into my new house, I had looked over the fence that divided my garden from my neighbour's and saw all the flowers that she had grown and that had matured over the years. 'How I would love to have a garden like that' I had said to myself, and so I decided to take the bus to town to buy flowers that would make my garden look just like hers.

"I will have six of those," I said to the man at the market stall, not knowing what 'they' were, but thinking the picture on the box looked nice; then to Woolworth's where I bought a stick that will grow (so it says on the packet), six feet tall with lovely pink flowers. That's for me

I say as I made my way home, imagining that soon my garden would look just like the one over the fence.

So I had planted my flowers and then my stick. I then stood back to admire the work of my day, looking forward to summer and seeing my 6-ft bush with lovely pink flowers and blooms that would soon stand in a vase where everyone that came to the house would stand back and admire, saying 'did you really grow those yourself?'

Soon summer came and the days were warm but standing looking out of my kitchen window at six plants, which I had planted at the end of my 50-ft garden, they were nowhere to be seen. My stick that promised to grow 6-ft tall with lovely pink flowers was still a stick and as I gazed at the garden over the fence I had said to myself 'my garden will never be like yours.'

Now the years have gone by and my neighbour is no longer there and her flowers have all withered and died. But now as I look out my kitchen window, I see a garden that has matured and a bush that has grown 6-ft tall with pretty pink flowers and then I remember my grandson and the joy that one new spring flower gave him. So, grabbing a watering can and filling it with water, I call to him "come over here, let's give the flower a drink," and as I see his face light up with the smile of spring, I remember my six of those and my stick that will grow 6-ft tall with lovely pink flowers and I grin.

2

NINE O'CLOCK

Nine o'clock, is that what the time is? I yawn and stretch not really looking forward to the night ahead, but there is no changing my mind as I had promised to do the extra shift. Was it only a few hours earlier that, at 1.30 in the afternoon after shopping, ironing, drinking tea and eating toast, I had crawled beneath the sheets, pulling the duvet over my head longing for sleep? But sleep was a long time coming, for all I could do was think on the night before. How many times, I asked myself, had I run up and down stairs to change beds, get a hot drink, or a glass of water and at one time just sitting, listening to the phrase "*when I was young*." "When I was young," oh what memories that phrase must conjure up: "When I was young."

Being young isn't too long ago for me, but for the residents (though I like to call them friends), how long ago for them - 50, 60 years? As I look at photos sitting proudly on the cupboards at the side of their beds, a young man or woman on their arm, or with children all smiling, and probably saying cheese, having their photo taken while out on a summer's day. I look at them and I don't see them as they are now, but see them as they were then. Even if their years are old and their skin no longer has the look of youth, there is still the smile that greets me each night and the question "Are you ok?; been looking forward to seeing you. Did you have a good sleep?" Then my heart goes out to them and I think to myself, will there come a time when I will say "when I was young?" Now I look at the clock and its ten past nine and time to get up, so sitting and dangling my legs over the bed I slowly stand and think to myself "I can't jump out of bed like I used to …"when I was young."

3

MY LITTLE SECRET

"You look smart" said a friend who I had not seen for while. "Mind you, you always look smart."

"Thank you" I said.

"You will have to tell me where you shop?"

"Oh here and there wherever the bargains are," I reply with a smile.

"I too look for the bargains but I must be looking in the wrong place" she says with the tone of disappointment. "It's been nice seeing you again, but I must be going, lots to do."

Should I have told her about my favourite shops I wonder, but no, that is my little secret; still it was nice of her to say how I always looked smart.

"Hallo, how are you" I am asked, as someone pokes me on the shoulder "have you been away?"

"Oh hallo" I say, staring at someone whose face I know, but can't remember the name.

"Shopping are you?" she asks.

"Not really, just looking around for the bargains."

"Well you must always find them as you always look nice."

"Thank you," I reply. "They're there, for all to find, you just have to be in the right place at the right time."

"Well that lets me out" she said, laughing. "I'm never in the right place at the right time."

"Sorry, can't stay and talk; just on my way to collect the children. I do wish they would stay in school for their dinner. That's probably why I'm never in the right place at the right time."

Should I have told her where to look for the bargains? It was kind of her to say I always look nice, but no that is my little secret.

Now I'm thinking I'll start at the bottom end of the high street today; that will make a change, and then work my way up to the top, then cross the road, and back down the other side. That way I'll be sure not to miss any of my favourite shops.

I wonder what bargains I will find today.

"Hallo, nice to see you. Is that one of ours? It really suits you! We had lots of donations in lately, I'm sure you will find something you like." and so I begin to scour the rails, looking first for the size on the hanger (that's my little secret), but I am not looking for anything in particular so when I find it, it will be a surprise, and so I search first among the skirts, then the blouses, now the jackets, hanging alongside the coats. Hallo! There are the trousers, all standing to attention, saying 'buy me.'

"But not today," I answer, as I search among the china, curtains, toys, and books. I am not disappointed though, as there are many more of my favourite charity shops, which is my little secret, up and down the high street.

4

OH, THAT'S MARVELOUS

"MARVELOUS" How does the dictionary describe this word? *Amazing, Astonishing, Extraordinary, Miraculous, Strange and Wonderful.*

But really, something marvellous is in the eye of the one that either feels, sees, hears or even touches.

To the young child growing up, everything is marvellous, as they look around their world they see and hear things that they have never seen nor heard before. The sound of a voice; the smile that tells them that everything is alright. The sight and sound of trees blowing in the wind; their first flower, and the touch of the kitten that only wants to play.

To the teenager, it's the music they hear or the dance that is new; the fashion they see which says "you must have me," and then the boy who looks at them from across the room and the feeling which says 'this is something new.'

To the young man or woman, it is the joy of exploring the world, visiting places they never thought to see... the Pyramids and the wonders that lie beneath; the Taj Mahal, which was built out of love... the Statue of Liberty, which was given as a gift to a nation.

To those who are married, the joy of a home, of children, the good times and the bad; the highs and lows and of saying "I knew it would turn out alright in the end."

And to those in their twilight years, remembering and asking "where has the time gone?" Wishing and yearning to have those years back again and promising to do things differently next time. Then memory takes over and a smile in place of a frown as the sound of a child brings joy to the heart and music to the ear as they tap the ground. "Times have changed" they hear someone say, but the Pyramids arc still there and the Lady Liberty too. So we have not changed, only you.

5

BREAKDOWN ON THE SIX FORTY FIVE

Phew, thought I was going to miss you today, well at least this carriage is not too full. Now where shall I sit?

"No, no, it's ok thank you." It was polite of that man to offer me a seat; I hope he wasn't offended by my saying no, but I prefer to sit over there by the window. I do like to sit on my own when I have the chance. Six forty-five by my watch; the train should be leaving now.

Not sure what I'm going to have to eat tonight, wish I could have popped out at dinnertime to get something; can't understand why we were so busy at work today; Wednesdays are not normally busy. I suppose because of the bank holiday - that's made a difference.

"Oh sorry," oh dear, I didn't realise my computer was poking out so much, but I have to put it under the seat as it's too heavy to keep on my lap. Hope he's ok. Knocking your ankle on a computer can be painful. I know. Better push it back further. Mind you, he did give me a smile, so maybe it didn't hurt too much.

Surely this train should be moving by now; it's seven o'clock by my watch. I'll try to look at the watch on that woman's arm in case mine, for some reason, is not right.

No - can't quite see it under the sleeve of her coat. I do like her coat; it looks much too expensive for my pocket. I could ask for a raise, but I don't think I'll get one. Not keen on her shoes though; don't think I would of worn THEM with that coat.

Mind I do like the shoes the woman sitting next to her has on; they would go much better with the coat. I wonder if I mentioned it, would they swap shoes.

Ten past seven - what's going on? Maybe the train driver has not turned up, perhaps he overslept; do they work all night, I wonder? I don't think I would like to be a train driver - it must be very boring, sitting in the driver's cab all on your own with no one to talk too. I wonder if he listens to music. Could he drive and listen to music at the same time; they may have rules against doing that.

Oh come on driver, I want to get home.

Oh, what's that? Is that someone speaking over the tannoy? What did he say? I'm sure I heard something about a train broken down; I hope that doesn't mean us. I'll ask that nice man who offered me the seat.

"Excuse me, I didn't quite hear the announcement, do you know what was said?"

"Oh, you didn't hear it either. Oh well thank you anyway."

He does have a lovely smile; I wonder if he's married.

No one's getting up to leave the train so at least I don't have to move, not that the view from this window is anything special, but I'm too tired to move anyway.

That baby's getting restless; I wonder how old it is. Must be a boy, as it's dressed all in blue; wonder why we put blue on a boy and pink on a girl? We do dress girls in blue but never seem to dress boys in pink! What is the mum looking for in her bag? Oh, a bottle of milk - should have guessed!

If the train has broken down, will we have to wait until the train is mended, or will they tow it away? Do they tow trains away? I never really thought about that one. Maybe they just change the engine.

The baby's settled; that's good.

Twenty past seven already, don't they know I just want to get home? I really could do with a cup of tea. I wonder if that man drinks tea, he looks more like some one who will go home to a glass of sherry. Looks like a bank manager; do bank managers go home to a cup of tea? I wonder if he would give me a loan, then may be I could buy a coat. I do like that coat.

Probably lives in a big house in the city with two cars in the garage. I wonder why he uses the train. He must be able to afford to run his cars; still, I suppose using the train is easier than driving through all the traffic, especially in the rush hour. Every hour is rush hour these days. Didn't I see a program about people having to sit in their cars for ages because of the traffic jams? Maybe it's a good job, I don't have a car. Still, if I did, I wouldn't drive it to work.

Where would I go in my car? It would be easier to get to see Mum; must phone her when I get in. I think I'll wait till after I've had my tea, as she does like to spend a while on the phone. Oh, just remembered, I think she's going to visit my sister this evening. I wonder how she is; it must be hard starting work again after bringing up a family; still, very capable is my sister.

Did the train move then? There it goes again, it *was* - the train is moving - cup of tea here I come! Oh, it's stopped again! Come on, come on, you can do it, move!

What's that say on the front of that newspaper? I wish she would hold it up higher so I can read it? NO, NO, don't put it away! I haven't read it yet - just a bit higher. Now move your hand, I can just about see what it says.

"LEAVES ON RAILWAY LINE HALTS TRAIN."

You're kidding me!

6

IN THE CORNER OF MY GARDEN

"Sally, where are you?" called Mum from the sitting room that was part of a house situated alongside a busy main road.

The people that now lived there had at one time lived in a much quieter suburb, but when Sally's grandmother (who had bought the house when she was first married) had become ill, it was decided that Sally's Mum, the only child of her grandmother, would move back into the home where she grew up, taking her family with her.

At first it had seemed that Sally would never settle, for she missed not only her school and the friends she had made from her early years, but the bench in the far corner of her garden, where she would sit and daydream; thinking about all the things she would do when she grew up.

She had often asked herself why it was that she would go to the corner of the garden and sit on the bench and daydream. Not like her friends, who would lay on their beds. Was it, she wondered, the sound of the birds that settled in the large sycamore tree, and how she would listen to their songs as she leaned back, closing her eyes, living the many adventures that one day she hoped she would have. Her Dad had threatened so many times to have the tree chopped down, saying "it stops the sun from reaching the corner of the garden," but she secretly new that her Dad loved the tree as much as she did. Was it still standing, she wondered; maybe the people who now lived there had decided they wanted more sun for the corner of the garden.

Oh how she missed that tree! There was no tree where she lived now, for the garden was small, with just a few flowers planted along the fence that divided the house from the neighbour's. How could her grandma have lived in this house for so long? And especially with a garden that has no tree, she had often asked herself.

"Sally, where are you" her Mother called again.

"Coming" Sally shouted from the top of the stairs.

"Why are you spending so much of your time in your bedroom, you should be out in the garden; why don't you go and sit on Granma's bench - she would love to think that you were sitting there and enjoying that corner of the garden just like she did" her Mother asked.

"I miss Grandma and sitting on her bench just doesn't feel right," answered Sally. Her Mother stood looking at her young daughter and for a moment she too felt an overwhelming loss for her Mother, but realised that the child who stood in front of her was missing her Grandmother more than she had appreciated.

"I have something for you" her Mother said, as she walked towards the dresser that stood against the wall. Then opening one of the drawers, she took out what looked like a biscuit tin. Looking at the tin, which had a lid that showed pictures of all different biscuits, Sally thought for a moment that her Mother, who normally only allowed her to have a biscuit after her dinner, felt sorry for her, so was allowing her to have a treat this one time.

"This is for you," said her Mother, handing her the tin. "Grandma said I would know when the time was right for you to have it. I was going to give it to you when you were older but maybe the time is right now. Take it out to the corner of the garden".

Looking at the tin, Sally felt just for a moment her heart skip a beat, wondering what was inside that her Grandma wanted her to have. So, taking the tin, she strolled towards the bench but decided when she got there she still did not want to sit on "Grandma's bench." Instead, kneeling down on the grass, which felt warm from the sun, she once more looked at the tin and began to wonder what she would find inside.

Slowly she began to ease the lid, which came off far easier than she had expected and placing the lid on the grass beside her, she began to take out, one by one, the items that stared back at her.

She gently laid each item on the grass. First the two little boxes, then the two folded pieces of paper; a locket that had a fine delicate chain which was not as shiny as the one that her Mum had bought her and then a letter with her name written on the envelope, which she knew by the handwriting, was from her Grandma.

Should she open the letter first she wondered, as she looked at each of the items that she had so gently placed in front of her. The letter might make me sad and I don't want to be sad, she thought. So turning towards the two pieces of folded paper she picked the first one up and as she opened it she noticed that at the top of the paper was her Mother's name and alongside was written 'aged 5 years.' Even more curious, she quickly opened the folded paper and staring at her was a drawing of a garden with different coloured flowers growing alongside a fence, but the flowers were not all as they should be, for they were the work of some one young who had not yet learnt where the leaves should go and did flowers really look like that? But there in the corner of the garden stood what looked like a bench and she was sure that someone was sitting there.

She stared looking at the drawing. Did her Mother really draw this all of those years ago, she thought. Now she couldn't wait to open the second piece of paper, but what a surprise she got, for written at the top was her name. 'Sally aged 6,' and her picture too was of a garden with flowers that were not drawn as they should be, for the leaves were all in the wrong place and do flowers really looked like that? And there was her tree and underneath, was that a drawing of her bench she wondered, where she would sit and daydream and as she laid the drawings on the grass, she decided it was the two little boxes that she would open next.

She lifted the lids and there, wrapped inside each box, was a delicate lock of hair, almost identical in colour. As she held each lid she noticed that once again, written on them was hers and her Mother's name.

Now the locket, she thought, almost too frightened to pick it up. The colour was gold with a pattern on the top that had almost faded. How lovely it is, she thought, as she gently held it in her hand. Would this one open as the one her Mother had given her she wondered. Inside hers was a photo of her Mother which she knew she would always keep, and an inscription which said "Remember I am always with you." Turning it to its side she noticed a small clasp, and then very carefully she eased the lock open. Who is this, she wondered, as she gazed at the face of a young man in the small black and white photo. Who is this and why did Granma keep it in the tin?

She was about to lay it down on the grass when she noticed the writing on the other side of the open locket. Holding the locket close she began to read the words which again were almost faded. "Remember I am always with you."

Lastly, picking up the envelope, she held it for a moment in her hand before carefully breaking the seal, then taking the letter from inside she began to read.

My dearest Sally,

This is a tin full of my treasures that I have kept for you. They are treasures that I have kept close to my heart for many years and why they are treasures is because they are treasures that can never be replaced. The first drawing, as you have found out, was drawn by your Mother on her first day at school. Even now all these years later, I can still see the smile on her face as she handed me her drawing "it's a picture of my garden Mummy; there flowers and that's the bench where we sit" she said, pointing at the drawing and hopping from one foot to the other. Now to your drawing. Do you remember the day you gave it to me? It was a picture of your garden, of flowers and the tree that you loved, the bench where you sat and dreamed. I remember too the smile that you gave as you handed me your picture, saying "this is for you grandma." So this too is a treasure which can never be replaced.

The locks of hair are from you and your Mother. Have you noticed how so much alike they are? When I first held you in my arms I thought I was holding your Mother all over again, and was that a smile I saw as I looked at your tiny face? But would I forget as I grew older I asked myself, of how small you both were and the joy that you both gave me, so if I forget, I can open my tin and remember.

14

Now the locket, given to me many years before you were born, in fact before even you're Mother was born. It was given to me by your Grandfather on the day that we were married. I did intend at first to give it to your Mother, but you were so very young when he died, you never really knew him. That is why I have decided to give it to you. I have tried to make him live on in your heart by telling you as much as I could about him but the locket along with my memories, is all that I can leave you.

So you see all these things that I have given to you are treasures, along with my memories, that can never be replaced but remembered.

"I am always with you".

Grandma

Sally slowly put the letter back in the envelope, then one by one returned each gift to the tin and then, as she closed the lid, she held it to her and getting up made her way to the bench in the corner of the garden, where her Grandma must have sat many times and thought about her treasures.

7

THE HOLIDAY

"Morning," Miss Smith called out with a smile as she opened the door to a classroom full of noisy children. "Weekend over it's time to settle down." Sitting at her desk and opening the register she began to call out their names, hoping that all in her class would be present. She noticed, as she marked each child with a red tick as they shouted "here miss," the number of black crosses that stood out on the page in front of her and hoped that the colds that had seen almost half her class empty over the last few weeks was now subsiding. Much better this week, she thought - lots more red ticks.

When she had first decided to teach, it was suggested to her by her parents that maybe teaching older children, perhaps in the range of fourteen or fifteen years old, would be more challenging for her but she new from the start that her heart laid with children a little younger, who's curiosity would not only stir her imagination by living in there world but also bring many a smile to her face.

Register over, she looked around at the eyes all staring back at her, wishing that summer was near so the greyness of winter would no longer tell on their young faces.

Could winter really have that effect she wondered? She had always made sure that her class had plenty of exercise. She could hear herself now shouting when it was her turn to supervise at play time 'come on run around, or stamp your feet, clap your hands, keep moving, you won't feel the cold then.' Did they think she was a nag; she asked herself and just for a second wondered what her class really thought of her?

Her daydreaming was suddenly interrupted by laughter coming from a group of children who seemed oblivious to the fact that it was Monday morning and the weekend was over.

"What's going on then?" she said, trying to sound just a little annoyed. Silence fell, "Billy's been making us laugh miss." "Is that so," she said, looking towards Kelly, who wasn't one of the quietest in the class. "Well let's all join in the joke Billy" she said, again trying to sound a little annoyed and it was then that she remembered that Billy had not been one of those that had not attended school because of a cold but had been given permission to take a week's holiday in the middle of term.

"Just telling some of the things that happened on my holiday Miss."

"Well, let's all hear them, so we can all join in," she said, trying once again to sound just a little irritated.

"You might not think it's funny Miss" Billy answered with the cheeky grin he always seemed to have on his face.

"Try me" were her next words.

"Well, Dad wanted to go to South End as that's where he grew up, but Mum didn't want to, she wanted to go to Spain - said she wanted the sun and sandy beaches, not rain and pebbles. Me? I didn't mind; I just wanted a holiday."

"Hope that doesn't mean you don't like school Billy" which made all the children laugh.

"Course not Miss, I love school" answered Billy and at the same time winking at Kelly.

"Anyway," Billy continued "Mum and Dad decided to toss a coin; heads we go to Spain, tails we go to South End.

Miss Smith looked around her class and her heart gave a little leap, which brought a smile to her face as she looked at each of the faces that were eagerly awaiting the outcome of the coin toss.

"I remember," said Billy, watching the coin being flicked into the air, thinking 'coo didn't know that Dad could flick a coin that high, I'll have to try that.'

"Where did you go? Where did you go?" shouted the children eagerly, awaiting the outcome on which way the coin had landed.

"South End."

"Oh" was the response from most of the class; obvious from the tone they wanted Spain.

"Where's South End Miss?" Tommy asked.

"About fifty miles from London, I think" she answered "and its proper name is South End-on-Sea. It's situated in an area of England known as Essex."

"Don't know about that Miss," said Billy "but it was lovely."

"Did it rain?" shouted Jimmy, making all the children laugh.

"Yes but not all the time. Anyway, there was so much to do it didn't matter."

"What did you do, what did you do" shouted Kelly.

"Don't shout Kelly," Billy can hear you without shouting" Miss Smith said and turning towards Billy, she asked "did you know much about South End-on-Sea before you went, Billy?"

"No Miss" Billy replied.

"Well it was over 150 years ago that a railway line was built from London to South End, and of course once that happened, people started to go there all the time for their holiday."

"I went by car Miss, not by train" Billy said with the tone that sounded as if it would be a crime to go by train.

"What car you got then," asked Tommy.

"Talk about the car another time; carry on Billy," Miss Smith said smiling.

"Forgot where I was Miss"   Billy said, frowning.

"Tell us about the things you did and the places you visited" said Miss Smith.

"Well, we first went to the pier, as Dad said he used to go there all the time when he was a boy. He said it was over a mile long; it's got a railway and a museum; we had ice cream, and there were people fishing as well."

"I don't like fishing Miss" Kelly said.

"The pier has quite a history Billy, perhaps we can spend a little time talking more about it in one of our history lessons, but carry on" Miss Smith said, while watching Tommy out of the corner of her eye, as she felt sure he was now pulling the hair of the girl who sat in front of him. Tommy, realising he was being watched, quickly put his hand under the desk. 'You look as if butter wouldn't melt in your mouth Tommy,' Miss Smith thought, secretly smiling inside.

"We went to an adventure park where there were loads of rides, some of them really scary. I wasn't scared, mind."

"Bet you was" said Tommy.

"No I was not," Billy said, putting on a brave face.

"I would have been scared," said Kelly "and I don't mind saying so."

Did you swim in the sea" asked Jimmy. "When I went to Spain, I could feel all the fish swimming around my legs; it felt really funny."

"When did you go to Spain? I never knew you went to Spain," asked Tommy.

"I did too, last time we went away" answered Jimmy, standing up.

"Sit down Jimmy and you stop teasing him Tommy, you know very well Jimmy went to Spain you had enough to say about it when Jimmy was telling us all about his holiday," Miss Smith said, sounding as if she really was cross this time.

"Did you swim in the sea" Miss Smith asked.

"No it was too cold, but I did so much Miss, and there was a still lot to do, but the week went so fast and then we had to come home."

With that the sound of a bell that said playtime was about to start was ringing in everyone's ears and no longer did it seem that the class was interested in Billy's holiday, for all the children were now eager to get out and onto the playground. "Alright everybody, I'm sure we would like to thank Billy for telling us about his holiday, and though we have not heard all of what he has to say, you can go on asking him questions."

Walking towards the classroom door, Miss Smith raised her voice, saying "all in a straight line now, and make your way slowly outside; no pushing or shoving."

Scrambling to be first, each child made their way outside, and as their chatter slowly died away and because it was not her turn to supervise the playground, she sat quietly in her chair before making her way to the staff room. 'What a good way to begin the week' she thought. 'Billy's holiday had got everyone off to a fine start and there will be plenty to talk about in their next history lesson.' 'South End-on-Sea' she thought a small part of the British Isles, yet a place with so much history even she would have to do her homework. Then, looking around her empty classroom she could still hear the laughter and the chatter of her class and knew that she had made the right decision in teaching ones a little younger than 14 or 15, for she had become part of their world and their imaginations, and she loved it.

8

THE TABLES TURNED

"Are you going to take me shopping or not?" a voice called from the kitchen.

"I said I would, didn't I?" an irritated voice called back from the sitting room of a three bed roomed house situated about a 15 minute car ride from the nearest town, at least that was on a good day when most cars were still parked in their garages.

"Well it's only that I promised the children we would be home in plenty of time, so we could all have an early tea, as there's something they want to watch on television," the voice from the kitchen answered, this time sounding just a little impatient.

"Why can't they watch it on their own television, and beside why do you always insist on calling them 'children?' Your son is nearly 25 and his wife was never one of our children" the voice from the sitting room replied, sounding even more irritated.

Having made her way from the kitchen to the sitting room she now stood in front of him, tall and elegant in her 2 inch heals; the navy skirt she wore was not like the ones that seemed popular at the moment, almost touching the ground but always stayed faithful to 4 inches below the knee. With a long sleeved white blouse tucked in at her waist that had not grown too much over the years considering she had had three children. With a jacket that matched her skirt, she looked more like an efficient business women who was on her way to the office, instead of going to town to shop on a Saturday afternoon.

So far only one of her sons had married, with the other two deciding that they would leave the family home and fend for themselves. She had always believed that bringing the children up as independent as she could would be a good thing, but sometimes in her quiet moments had wondered whether she had perhaps taught them to be just a little *too* independent, as she so often missed them. They did visit whenever

they could, but there was always that empty feeling inside of her when she waved goodbye as they left.

"Oh stop being so grumpy, you've been like it since you got up. A good dose of salts that's what you need."

Why on earth had she said that, she wondered? "A good dose of salts, that's what you need my girl; you have been nothing but a misery all day." How many times in her childhood had she heard her Mum say those same words? She could see her now, standing at the sink with both hands in water; then, as she turned lifting one hand and pointing her finger at her, she would watch as the trail of water ran down her hand and then down her arm till it reached her elbow and then dripped to the floor. The things we remember, she said to herself.

"Come on get your coat on, the sooner we get out the sooner we'll be back" she said, making her way to the front door.

"I don't know why I have to come, why you can't take the car and go on your own I don't know" he continued, as he reluctantly eased himself out of his chair.

Why was he feeling so bad tempered, he wondered - it wasn't that he had had a late night, perhaps it was the cheese sandwich he ate before going to bed. Why was she always right he thought, as he recalled her words "if you eat that, you'll be grumpy tomorrow." "Does she know me that well?" That was a question he had asked himself many times over the years.

Reluctantly he made his way to the front door, grabbing his coat and car keys from the hall stand and as he did so, he glanced at himself in the mirror, then just for a second stopped as he stared at the face that was looking back at him.

"Mm, you don't look too bad for your age, nobody would think you have three grown up sons, and I like that hint of grey hair each side of your head - makes you look rather distinguished, and not too many wrinkles yet. You're doing all right!" he said quietly to himself, raising one eyebrow and puffing out his chest as he did so.

"Are you ready?" his wife called as she stood next to the car. "I can't get in till you've opened the door."

"Alright, alright, I'm coming" he shouted back, the spell broken.

Closing the front door behind him he made his way to the car.

"Did you put the alarm on?" she asked.

"Of course I put the alarm on" he replied, but wondered, 'did I?'

'I do hope traffic into town is not going to be too bad' she says to herself, 'he's in such a mood now, perhaps I should have said I would go on my own, I did warn him about eating that cheese sandwich before going to bed.'

As he pulled out of the drive way and onto the road he asked "How much shopping have you got to do?"

Thinking quickly, she answers "not too much, if we can go to the supermarket I can get most of what I want there; don't worry I'm not going to drag you around the shops."

"Well the traffic isn't too bad, so at least that's one thing in our favour" he says, his tone not quite so grumpy.

'Mood getting better' she thought.

"Did they say what they wanted to watch on television?" he asked.

"No, just said they wanted to come over and watch a program on our television."

"Mm" was his reply.

"Now what?" he asked, as he began to slow the engine down, finally stopping as he found himself in a queue of traffic. "Can you see what's holding us up from your side" he asked.

Rolling down the window she looked to the front of the queue.

"It looks as if there is only one car involved and I can see two people and children standing on the pavement; I do hope there's not been an accident" she said, with concern in her voice.

"Well if it is an accident the police and ambulance will be here soon and then we can be on our way" to which she turned towards him thinking 'I can't believe you just said that.' "There's the police car now" he said, hearing the sound of the siren as it approached "can't see an ambulance though."

"Good, that means no one's hurt" she said with a sigh of relief in her voice.

"What's happening now?" he asked, while tapping his fingers on the steering wheel, sighing as he did.

"I don't know, the policeman is talking to the man, but the woman seems very agitated, probably worried about the children." Soon five minutes had gone by then ten and the tapping on the steering wheel began to get quicker and the sighing louder, but she pretended not to notice.

"I don't believe it," "I don't believe it" he said, breaking the silence.

"What don't you believe?" she asked.

"That policeman, he's only talking to the drivers in the cars, so it's taking up more time."

"Well he's probably thanking every one for there patience" she answered, with just a slight hint of sarcasm in her voice.

"The breakdown lorry has finally arrived; I can see the lights flashing on the lorry" he said, pretending he didn't know what she was hinting at.

"Well at least we won't have to wait too long now. In fact, it looks as if the cars in front are beginning to move" she said, smiling at him,

24

knowing that the tapping on the steering wheel would finally stop.

"Why don't people have their cars serviced regularly? Then they would not end up stopping in the middle of a high street holding all the traffic up" he said, his bad mood returning. "Good thing the police turned up when they did, or we'd be sitting here all day" he continued.

Then as she watched him reach toward the key, just for a moment; she wished that when he turned it, the engine would not start.

'I can't believe I thought that' she said to herself, with a grin on her face as the engine came to life and they slowly began to move. As they passed the broken down vehicle, she noticed how a sense of relief showed on the faces of the driver and his family now that help had arrived.

Then suddenly she saw not the car parked alongside the road, but the car that had once been his prize possession; the one she had pushed so many times when they were first courting. She could see herself first pushing it with her hands on the boot and then turning, trying to push it with her back as he shouted 'nearly there, 'nearly there,' as he ran alongside the open door and when the engine burst into life, he jumped into the car revving the engine as he sat with a grin on his face, patting the steering wheel saying 'good on you girl, good on you girl' as if the car understood every word he said. Had he forgotten those days she wondered?

The shopping over, they made their way home and this time the traffic flowed freely. Making sure he was the one to open the front door, he quickly jumped out of the car still hoping he had remembered to turn on the alarm then breathed a sigh of relief as the numbers are pushed. 'The things we do by habit,' he thought to himself as he made his way back to the car to help carry the shopping

"I'll put the kettle on while you put the shopping away; we could both do with a cup of tea" he said as he put the bags, full to the brim, on the kitchen table. Once the tea was made and with his cup in his hand he made his way to the sitting room and sat himself in his chair turned the television on, secretly hoping he wouldn't be called to help out in the kitchen.

"The food is nearly ready, I do hope it's not going to be too long before they get here" she said as she walked into the sitting room, looking just a little flushed from the heat of the cooking.

"That was quick" he said.

"Well you've been dozing; must have been that cheese sandwich you ate last night, or maybe all the excitement from the breakdown" she said, smiling at him.

Pretending not to notice the smile he said "Well, they know you are doing food for them so they shouldn't be too late" not mentioning the breakdown.

"What are you watching?" she asked, as his attention seemed to be drawn more to the television than to her.

"Just the news" he answered.

Making her way back to the kitchen, she checked the food once again and began to look for things to do; hoping it would take her mind off a reason the children could be late.

'He's right,' she thought to herself 'I shouldn't call them children, they're all grown up and maybe soon will have a family of their own,' then looking at the clock, she felt just a little anxious, knowing they should have been eating by now.

"What time did you say they would be here" he called the sound of the television no longer as loud as it was.

"They said round about six, but it's getting on for seven" she answered and as he heard the sound of concern in her voice this made him feel just a little apprehensive.

"You worry too much, they'll soon be here. They're most probably sitting in a queue of traffic because someone in front of them broke down, just because they never bothered to get their car serviced," he said, trying to cool her fears, but not sounding overly convincing.

'You're worried too; now I'm really worried if you're worried,' she said to herself as she walked back into the sitting room and toward the window hoping that when she looked out they would be pulling into the drive way.

"I'll phone them," she says, "perhaps they've forgotten that they are supposed to be coming."

'Typical,' he thought to himself but not saying it aloud, not wanting to add to her fear.

Lifting the phone and dialling their number, she stood letting it ring, waiting anxiously. "No reply" she said.

"There you are, they must be on their way, you worry for nothing," he said, trying to sound positive and now wishing he had not been in such a grumpy mood during the day. 'It must have been that cheese sandwich and that breakdown didn't help' he thought. 'Why oh why do people not look after their cars?'

Suddenly his thoughts were interrupted by the words 'they're here, they're here" and he felt a sudden surge of relief come over him as they both made their way to the front door.

"Where have you been, why are you so late" she asked, holding back the tears as she hugged them both "I was beginning to worry."

"Sorry Mum," her son answered, "we broke down."

"What do you mean you broke down? Don't you ever get that car of yours serviced?" he asked, sounding almost angry.

"Of course I do, but cars still break down, anyway, we didn't really break down, we just ran out of petrol."

"Ran out of petrol? What do you mean you ran out of petrol? Don't you ever check the gauge?"

27

"Come on Dad, I remember you telling us about your first car that was always breaking down and Mum having to push it" he said, laughing, as they all made their way to the sitting room. Then in a moment of time, he remembered his first car, the one that had been his prize possession and how he had polished it with pride. The times they had both spent pushing it, for he was always running out of petrol as the gauge did not work. How many times had he phoned his Dad to come and tow him home as the engine had decided it didn't want to work that day, for he could never afford to have it serviced, not on his money! Then looking at his wife, he could see her now, pushing the car and him shouting 'nearly there, 'nearly there,' and the smile on her face as the engine burst into life and what was that he would say as he jumped into the car 'good on you girl, good on you girl,' as if the car understood every word he said and his heart filled with pride for the woman who had stayed faithful and said to himself 'I'll not be grumpy tomorrow.'

Now looking at his son, he could see himself as he was all those years ago and thought 'the tables have turned and will go on turning, as time never really changes anything' and knew that one day there may be a grandson who would remind his Dad of the day he ran out of petrol and broke down.

9

CATHERINE'S WHEEL

"Wake up, wake up; are you awake Catherine"? Said the sound of a voice that was slowly arousing Catherine from her sleep. "Catherine, can you hear me"? Catherine, slowly being made to end the sleep that she so desperately needed after finishing her late shift at the hospital, mumbled something like "yes, yes I'm awake" as she poked her head from under the duvet.

"The wheel on your car had a puncher; I've put the spare on but you will have to take it to the garage to put more air in the tyre, only it's a bit flat... got to go now, but I will see you after work. "Catherine, are you listening, did you hear me? Got to go or I'll be late for work."

"Yes, yes, I hear you. The car has a flat tyre and you will put the spare on when you come home from work, then you will put air in the tyre;" and with that Catherine rolled over and pulling the duvet back over her head and found the sleep that had been broken just a few moments earlier. Then no sooner it seemed that she had closed her eyes she was awakened by the alarm at the side of her bed.

Slowly, very slowly, she reluctantly opened her eyes to the sun that was casting its light through the drawn curtains, while thinking; I keep meaning to change those, they let in too much light. Then again, very slowly she began to pull herself up from the pillow that was still beckoning her. Sitting up she eased her legs from the warmth of the bed, slipping her feet into the slippers that were always left in the same place.

It was only then that she remembered that she had been woken from her sleep earlier, being told something about her car - or had she dreamt, it she wondered. No, something about a puncher and a wheel, and he will fix it when he comes home from work. Then put air in it. That's all I need, she thought.

Catherine made her way downstairs to make that first cup of tea of the day that she always looked forward too, hoping that by the time she had finished looking into the bottom of the cup she would be more like her old self, but somehow she knew that this morning would be different, since she had been told that the wheel on her car had a puncher.

Going to the window she looked out at the clouds that were beginning to gather, blocking out the sun that had shined so brightly when she had first woken up 'looks like it will rain before the day's out' she thought, and that will mean that Ben's going to get wet when he changes the tyre. Its times like this I wish we had a garage. Still, maybe one day, she said to herself with a sigh 'when my boat comes in.' How many times had she heard that saying she wondered. She could see herself now asking her Dad for something and he would answer "you can have it when my boat comes in," which meant she would soon have what it was that she'd asked for, and oh, how she had jumped up and down with excitement as the gift was given, thinking 'oh Dad's boat must have come in,' but then she had wondered where did Dad keep his boat? He had never taken her to see it. How many times have I wished my boat would come in she thought, but still I'm happy, so maybe my boat has come in after all?

'This won't do' she said to herself, getting up from her chair, having drunk the last dregs of tea; got lots to do.

After showering and dressing she decided to take a look at her car to make sure she had not been dreaming and that there really was a puncher. She made her way to the front of the house where the car was kept on the small driveway. It did not take her long to realise that it was not a dream after all, for the tyre that she looked at was indeed very low. "Oh dear" she said out loud, "I wont be able to use you today and I had planned to go shopping and I really don't fancy going by bus." Then, making her way back into the house, decided she would have another cup of tea. Tea is the answer to everything, she said to herself.

As she sat daydreaming, she suddenly thought, why can't I change the wheel instead of waiting for Ben to do it? Surely it can't be that hard. So with a new lease on life, she quickly finished her second cup of tea, then ran back up to her bedroom, taking the stairs two at a time, to change into clothes she would not mind getting dirty while feeling just a little excited. She began to imagine what Ben would say when she said

'It's alright, you don't need to change the wheel, I've done it' and then to see the surprised look on his face.

Standing by the car she looked at the wheel. Now, she thought, the first thing I know I have to do is lift the wheel of the ground. So going to the boot where she knows the jack which will lift the car is kept, she slowly takes out first a shopping trolley, then carrier bags, then an empty petrol can; next a first aid kit, then an old sack which she remembered she had used to take rubbish to the council tip in, and then an old blanket and at last, beneath all this, she saw the jack. At last, she thought. Turning to climb over all the things she'd taken out of the boot she noticed a pair of eyes watching her.

"What you doing?" the young voice asked, which she soon realised was coming from the little girl who lived next door. "I'm looking for the jack that will help me lift the car, so I can change the wheel, as I have a puncture" said Catherine.

"Jack's indoors" said the young voice; "anyway he's too young to change a wheel." Catherine, suddenly remembering that Jack was the name of the new baby said "no not *your* Jack, jack is the name of the tool that will help lift my car.

"Why do they call it jack?" she was asked again. "I don't know, anyway you stand back now, I don't want you to get hurt," Catherine answered, secretly hoping that no more questions would be asked.

After lifting the jack from the boot she made her way to the side of the car then bending down she began to look for the place where she knew the jack would have to be secured. First she moved it to the left and then to the right, but still was unsure where it should go, next she found herself almost lying on the ground - it's got to go somewhere, she thought.

"Are you all right?" a voice asked. Slowly turning, she saw the elderly couple who lived two doors down from her, standing and watching.

"She's looking for jack to mend her wheel" said the young girl, to which the elderly couple smiled. Catherine, a bit frustrated by now said "I'm trying to find the safest place to put the jack."

"Sometimes" said the elderly man, "there is a small ring that the jack fits into; move your fingers up and down the edge of the car." Turning back Catherine began to do as the elderly man had suggested and soon she shouted "I've found it, I've found it, it's here," then slowly getting up from the ground and kneeling, she eases the jack into the small hole.

"Now turn the handle" said the elderly man as his wife stood smiling.

It was not long before the side of the car was lifted from the ground.

"Did you loosen the bolts of the wheel first"? the elderly man asked.

"No, should I have done?" Catherine asked, her confidence slowly slipping away.

"Yes, you'll have to lower the car now, to undo the bolts," came the reply.

Gradually the car was lowered and then the elderly man said "you will need a wheel brace to undo the bolts".

"What is a wheel brace?" The question she really wished she didn't have to ask.

"It's what's used to loosen the bolts. You should have one in your boot; I'm sure your husband would keep it in there in case of emergencies."

Looking into the boot again she noticed tucked in the corner what she thought was the wheel brace.

"Is this it?" she asked, showing the tool to the elderly man.

"Yes that's it; now all that needs doing is to loosen the bolts. Would you like me to do that for you?" he asked.

"No, no, I'm sure it's easy enough, I'm sure I can do it."

Slowly she fitted the end of the brace onto the bolt and began. She hoped to turn the bolt, but even as she struggled, the bolt would not turn; instead the brace left the bolt.

"Are you ok?" the elderly woman asked, while the young child laughed thinking it was funny to suddenly see Catherine lurch forward? 'This is going to be harder than I thought she said to herself,' secretly wishing that she had waited for Ben who would have probably changed the wheel in five minuets and without an audience. Trying again, she only managed to turn the bolt slightly when she again was asked "Do you need any help?" Before looking up she noticed a pair of working boots pointing towards her and then remembered that the house across the road to her was having their roof repaired, so the boots must belong to one of the workmen.

"She needs help getting the bolts off" said the elderly man.

"No. no, I'm sure I can do it" she said not really wanting to feel like a damsel in distress.

"Here let me have a go, Ill have them off in no time." Standing up she reluctantly handed the builder the brace and stood alongside the elderly couple and the small child who, by this time, seemed fascinated by the little play that had taken place. But the builder had been right, for in no time at all the bolts had been loosened and the car had once again been lifted; then the spare wheel had been bolted into place; but standing back and looking at the wheel the builder said "you need to put some air in that tyre, it looks nearly flat to me".

"Yes I know" said Catherine, "before my husband left for work this morning he said I would need to put air in the tyre; I'll drive the car to the garage now."

Catherine thanked the builder and the elderly couple for all their help and saying to the little girl that she should go home and that she would see her again, closed the front door and made her way back to the car and was soon driving very slowly to the garage, knowing that soon the tyre wood look as good a new, and she would feel pleased with herself for the rest of the day.

Hearing Ben's key in the door she began to feel excited: he would never believe that she had changed the wheel of the car, and she couldn't wait to tell him.

"How's your day been?" Ben asked as he walked through the door, did you not have time to go to the garage and put air in the tyre?"

"Yes I put air in the tyre; in fact I've saved you a job, I changed the wheel!" Ben stood staring at her, not really understanding for a moment what she had said.

"What do you mean you changed the wheel?" Ben asked again.

"Well it was really quite fun in a way" she said, looking at Ben with a big grin on her face. "I decided that I would change the wheel myself and save you the job of doing it when you got home. Mind you I did have a little help from the elderly man two doors down, and then the builder came from across the road and he too gave me some help and of course I mustn't miss out the little girl from next door who thought that the whole episode was a laugh and that the jack was her brother," to which Ben frowned, not quite understanding what she meant. "But all in all," she said, waiting for the praise from Ben "I quite enjoyed it." Then she suddenly stopped and asked "what do you mean did I put air in the tyre? Yes of course I did."

Looking at her and listening to her enthusiasm he began to smile, and in his imagination he could see her beside the car surrounded by all the ones that she had spoken of, then very quietly not wanting to hurt her feelings said "I'm sorry, but I changed the wheel before I went to work, so you put the wheel with the puncture back on the car."

10

THE JOURNAL

"What you got there?" her Mum asked, as her daughter laid the card board box on the kitchen table "I hope it's not dirty."

"It was given to me by one of the sellers at the boot sale. The young woman who gave it to me said she didn't want to take it home again, as it would only sit in her garage."

"It looks like a load of junk to me, that's why," said her Mum, as she peered into the box. No one gives any thing good away these days."

"Oh stop being so negative Mum, you're always so negative."

"Have you rung Alfie yet?" her Mum asked, changing the subject.

"No," she answered, not really wanting to pursue that conversation, and felt relieved when her Mum did not make any more comments on that subject.

About to light the gas under the saucepan of potatoes, her Mum, looking in her direction said "take the box up to your bedroom and sort it out there, I'll call you when dinner's ready."

Lifting the box from the kitchen table she made her way to the stairs, glancing into the sitting room on the way, but saw no sign of her Dad; he must be in his shed she thought. She remembered always being told as a child that it was the place that Dads went for a bit of peace and quiet. "I'm going to my shed for a bit of peace and quiet, call me when foods ready" he had always said. Even times when she and her brother were not arguing he had still gone to his shed, but Mum never seemed to mind, always saying she was glad to get him out from under her feet. Would Alfie have wanted a garden shed where he could go for a bit of peace and quiet? She asked herself, but then quickly dismissed the thought from her mind as she opened her bedroom door.

Sitting on the side of the bed she was about to put the box beside her but then remembered it was just that morning that she had changed the bedding so decided the chair at the side of her bed would be a better place, just in case, she thought, remembering her Mum's words about the box being dirty. As soon as she had put the box down she leaned back onto her pillow and looking up at the ceiling, her thoughts turned to Alfie. Why hadn't he rung? Was he waiting for her to make the first move? Why is he so stubborn? And was it only a week ago that they had had words, and she had walked away; she felt sure that a week had never seemed so long - now she could hardly remember what they had argued about, but whatever it was she knew that SHE was not going to be the first one to ring.

Sitting up she pulled the chair a little closer to her, hoping that by going through the box it would take her mind off Alfie and after all, she was probably the last thing on HIS mind.

Peering into the box the first thing she saw was a rolling pin. Does anyone use rolling pins any more? She asked herself as she laid it on the bed beside her, first making sure it was clean. I think the last time I used one was when I was in school, she thought. She could see herself now standing behind the wooden table in the cookery class along with all the other girls, each with a rolling pin in their hand and the teacher saying "don't make the pastry too wet girls, or it will stick to the rolling pin."

"You should have put flower on the pin first before you rolled it out" she remembered her Mum saying as she looked at the soggy jam tart that was presented to her for tea. Oh Mum, she thought.

Next she took out a picture frame which she knew had seen better days – "that's for the bin" she said to herself, pulling a face. Then, tugging at a length of wire that had been resting on the frame, pulled to the top of the box a hair dryer which she felt sure did not work, for there was no plug attached to the end of the wire. Then, as she was about to bring out the next item, she heard her Mum calling, telling her that dinner was on the table and that she should come now.

As she walked into the kitchen, standing at the sink with his shirt sleeves rolled up and washing his hands was her Dad "You all right love?" he asked, "did you have a good time at the boot sale, buy anything nice?" "No" she answered; "I didn't buy anything this time, but was given a box full of bits and pieces by one of the seller's who didn't want to take it home."

"Looked like a load of junk to me" said her Mum taking off her apron before sitting at the table.

"Probably a box of treasure" said her Dad, looking at her and winking.

"Have you heard from Alfie?" he then asked her.

"No Dad" she replied "he's too stubborn to ring". To which her Mum and Dad looked at each other, having the same thought, but making no reply.

Dinner over she decided that instead of spending her time in the sitting room with her Mum and Dad she would finish emptying the box. Normally she loved Sunday afternoons, for it was a time that her family would sit together, her Dad reading the Sunday paper, knowing that by the time he got to the second page he would be fast asleep, snoring quietly, and her Mum checking the television program, hoping that there would be an old fashioned black and white film that would pull at the heart strings, making them both cry, but it would not be the same without Alfie she thought, who she knew only sat and watched the film to please her. He never laughed at her as he saw the tears running down her face - that was her Alfie.

"You coming to watch the telly?" her Mum asked, "I haven't checked to see if there's a black and white on yet," but before her Mum had finished her sentence she knew by the look on her daughter's face that the answer was going to be no.

"I think I will go up and finish emptying that box" she said knowing what her Mum's next question was going to be.

"Found any thing useful yet?" her Mum asked.

"No," she replied, "but there are a few more things in the box that I haven't gotten to yet," secretly knowing that before the week was out she would be making a trip to the rubbish tip and that her Mum had been right - it was just a box of junk after all.

Back upstairs once more her thoughts turned again to Alfie. They had known each other from their school days and at the time there had been nothing special about him, in fact she remembered that they had often teased each other. When their school years were finished they had gone their separate ways, but then while out shopping with her friend they had decided to go into a café for a coffee and looking around for a place to sit she had made her way to the table where the only two empty seats were. She had asked the boy sitting at the table if the seats were taken, only to realise that it was Alfie, who no longer was the boy she remembered from school, with his shirt always hanging out of his trousers, and with hair that was always too long and never looked combed. Oh how he had changed! Sitting in front of her was a young man dressed in a smart jacket that covered a clean white shirt, and was that a waistcoat under his jacket? She remembered thinking and his hair no longer had that uncombed look about it, for it was cut short in a neat modern style.

"Hello Alfie" she had said "do you remember me?" As he had looked at her she remembered how all of a sudden she had gotten tongue-tied, unable to finish her sentence. Was it then, she wondered, that she knew she loved him? When her friend had brought the coffees to the table she could not even remember introducing Alfie to her, or how long they sat at the table talking before she realised that somewhere between sentences her friend had said her goodbyes and left? Does love really happen that quickly, she wondered?

Turning back to the box, she again began taking out the items that were left: an empty tin, which did have a pretty picture on the lid but looked rusty round the edges; a wire coat hanger which she knew she would never use, as they always left a crease in her blouses, and even a pair of slippers which looked as if they had been well worn. Her Mum was right – no one gives away anything good these days.

She was about to put all the bits and pieces back in the box, thinking a trip to the rubbish tip was next on her agenda, when she noticed, tucked in the corner, a small reddish brown book. Taking it out she laid it on the bed beside her while looking at each item again as she refilled the box.

As she was about to pick up the book there was a knock at her door and walking in with a cup of tea was her Mum, with a concerned look on her face "are you ok?" she asked while handing her the cup.

"Yes I'm fine" she said, thanking her, hoping that her Mum would not bring up the subject of Alfie.

"You should ring you know," her Mum said, and was about to say something more but decided that perhaps this was not a good time. Then, giving her daughter a hug left the room, closing the door quietly behind her.

"Is she ok?" her Mum was asked as she entered the sitting room with cups of tea, this time in both hands. "I'm not sure" she replied as she laid the cups on the small table beside the settee and as she sat, ready to watch the Sunday film, she knew she secretly missed her daughter sitting next to her.

MY JOURNAL

Lifting the book she noticed how the letters on the front had faded, making it hard for her to read what she thought was the title. Gently rubbing the dust that had settled, she slowly began to make out each letter till the words,

My JOURNAL

appeared.

It was written in a delicate hand that she noticed was nothing like hers; with each letter carefully written. Once again she slowly ran her fingers over the cover, almost afraid to get to the first page, wondering what it was she was about to read. Slowly she opened the journal and felt sure that the person who had put pen to paper was about to open up to her a world that was so different from hers.

PAGE ONE OF THE JOURNAL

ARCHDUKE FRANZ FERDINAND AND HIS WIFE SOPHIE WERE KILLED ON THE 28th JUNE 1914.

THE GREAT WAR BEGAN ON THE 28th JULY 1914.

BRITIAN ENTERED THE WAR ON THE 4th AUGUST 1914.

CANADA ENTERED THE WAR ON THE 5th AUGUST 1914.

CANADIAN SOLDIERS ARRIVE ON BRITISH SOIL ON THE 14th OCTOBER1914.

THE GREAT WAR ENDED 11th NOVEMBER 1918.

What is this? She asked herself as she read the first page several times. Was it just a journal about the history of the First World War.? She remembered that there were times that this war had been mentioned in her school years, but she had no recollection that they had spent no more than just a few minuets from time to time talking about it. So, with a feeling of disappointment she turned over the page.

PAGES 2 AND 3

Pressed between the pages marked 2 and 3 was a leaf, faded now in colour but maybe with just a hint of red still there. Too frightened to touch it, just in case it crumbled in her hand, she turned the page.

PAGE 4

Staring at her was the face of a young man whose clean cut features showed strength, but with eyes that smiled, and as she looked closer, even though the drawing had almost faded, she was sure he was wearing a uniform.

PAGE 5

Turning the page there were just two words 'MY STORY.' Leaning back with her head propped up against her pillow, she slowly turned the page feeling her heart beating with anticipation at the story she was about to read.

PAGE 6

Why have I written all that I have on the pages before I start writing my journal? Is it to remind me of the time I lived in? A time when the world went mad; a time when we thought that the war we were fighting would be a war to end all wars, a war that would be over by Christmas. How many people died, and why did young men, some with wives and children, rush to put on a uniform?

About me: I am now 66 years old, living on my own. Two children I have and five grandchildren. I own my own home that has finally been paid for, and will one day be theirs. I grew up in a loving family with a Mum who stayed home but took in washing to help Dad, who worked hard to put food on the table and clothes on our backs. I had one younger brother who could not wait to put on his uniform and fight for his country, and then never came home. But the question I am now asking myself is: why am I writing all this down now? and the answer is, I do not know, but maybe my story starts many years ago.

In 1917 I was 21 years old, working hard in the local munitions factory (which I never expected to do), giving up my previous job as a housemaid to do my bit for our country, as we were encouraged to do, because the men were needed for the front line. I worked long hours, never begrudging what I was doing, for 'I was doing my bit.'

I remember the night in 1915 when my brother, my lovely brother, walked though the door with a big grin on his face and announced that he had joined up. Did he expect the reaction he got from my Mum and Dad? I'm sure that he did. "What do you want to do that for?" shouted Dad, as Mum lifted the piny she was wearing up to her face, shouting and sobbing "no, no, no" into it. "It's what I want to do" he said, "I'm no coward." It was not long after joining up that he proved he was no coward by giving his life.

My home for a long time after his death was a hard place to be and for a while even newspapers were banned in the house. Dad no longer whistled all the latest tunes and I can see my Mum now as I write, working around the house, not really knowing what she was doing, no longer smiling. I remember I would come home from work and there would be four places laid at the table instead of three, and Dad and I would pretend that we never noticed. It was as if someone had closed all the curtains in the house but they had forgotten to open them again to let the sunshine in.

Would life ever be normal again, I wondered; could the world ever be the way it was? There would never be another war, we were promised, but life could never be the same, for far too many lives had been lost and too many hearts had been broken.

How many months went by before my family pretended to be 'normal' again? I can't remember, but gradually my Mum smiled and no longer laid the table for four. I continued to work hard, and Dad began whistling again. Did they pretend it was normal just for me, I ask myself now. I don't know but how I loved them for that.

PAGE 7

"Are you coming to the dance tonight I was asked by the girl that was

working along side me?"

"No," I remember answering.

"Oh come on" she had said "it will do you good; it's been ages since we went out together - you'll enjoy it." I remember making all kinds of excuses but in the end I gave in and arranged to meet her inside the dance hall. I remember spending ages deciding what to wear, first choosing one thing, then changing my mind, but eventually deciding on a blue dress that had been tucked away in the back of the cupboard. It had been so long since I felt like going out, let alone dressing up, but I can still see the look on Dad's face when I walked into the kitchen and he looked up from reading one of the newspapers that had slowly made their way back into the house, saying "you look nice, where are you off too?" When I told him he smiled at me and said "about time you got out of the house and enjoyed yourself; have you got your door key?"

"Will you tell Mum I won't be late" I had replied.

"You go and enjoy yourself" he said again "don't worry about your Mum, it will be a while before she's in from next door, you know what its like when her and May get together, they can talk the hind leg of a donkey." Laughing, I grabbed my coat imagining Mum, May and the donkey. I would have loved to have a friend like May, I am thinking as I write. I can see her now walking towards the fire with a kettle in her hand and saying "shall I put the kettle on, and are you staying for tea?" Oh lovely May, how I miss you May.

PAGE 8

I remember taking off my coat and laying it on one of the long tables piled high with coats, hats and scarves and wondering how on earth I was going to find it when it was time to go home, but that was soon forgotten as I made my way towards the swing doors where I could hear the sound of music.

Pushing open the swing doors I remember looking around for my friend and wondering whether I would be able to find her among the crowds that were not only dancing but also standing around the dance floor, when suddenly a voice asked "are you looking for some one?" Turning, I saw standing behind me a tall young man dressed in an army uniform. "Its ok, I'm looking for my friend" I said, not really taking much notice of who it was asking the question. Then the music stopped, and before I had a chance to say any thing else I heard the voice of my friend calling me.

Soon I was being introduced to the person that was holding her hand. "This is Jimmy" she said "he works at our factory; you must have seen him around." Yes, I'm sure I have, I said and with that the band started playing again.

"Come on let's dance" said my friend grabbing hold of Jimmy's hand and pulling him toward the dance floor.

"Would you like to dance?" I was asked, "I'm not a brilliant dancer, but I think I can manage a waltz." I remember thinking, I know that voice but from where? And then I remembered - he was the young man who had spoken to me earlier. Taking hold of my hand, he led me to the dance floor and I can still hear the tune in my head that was playing "*Love will find a way*" and it did, for that was the start of a romance that has stayed hidden away in my memory all my years. But why, I ask myself do I remember now?

PAGE 9

He said his name was Jack and he was a soldier in the Canadian Army, enjoying his stay in England, but would be glad when the war was over and he could go home. I remember he wasn't handsome but had a mischievous glint in his eye that would light up his face when he smiled. I can't remember how many times we danced together that night, but by the end of the evening I felt that I had known him all my life. He asked if he could walk me home and then see me the following night, and that was the start of the romance.

It is so hard for me now to remember every minute that we spent together, but I know that each one that I do I have treasured. I remember, dear journal, how we laughed as he ran and caught an autumn leaf as it fell from the tree and said "this is for you," and when I took it from his hand I felt as if he had given me all the leaves in all of England. Then weeks would go by and I would never see him, with only his letters that told me he loved me and then the surprise when Dad said there's someone here to see you.

Mum and Dad liked him, but I *loved* him, and when he spoke about going home, I almost wished the war would never end. But the war did end, and as he kissed me goodbye. He would write, he said; he would send for me, he said and we would be married, but he never wrote and he never sent for me and we never married. I waited and waited, looking each day for the letter that said 'You're coming home' but it never came, and I don't know why, and I had waited so very long.

Now I must hide you away 'my journal,' for I share my secrets only with you, knowing that I will never have the answer, for not even you can tell me why he did not write and why he never sent for me; maybe he, too, had a secret.

THE END

About to shut the book she realised that there was still another page, but this time with out a page number. Quickly turning the page she began to read.

OBITUARY

Written by

"THE JOURNAL"

It is with deep regret that I announce the death of

JACK, HENRY, NELSON

Who died of the Spanish Flu on 31st January 1919

Closing the book and laying still on her pillow she realised she had tears in her eyes. If only there was some way she could make it right, she thought, but she knew there was nothing that she could do - it was all in the past. Was it true that it was better to have loved and lost than never have loved at all, she asked herself? She had never quite made up her mind over that saying. Then her thoughts returned to Alfie, and jumping up from her bed then running down the stairs, she grabbed her coat while shouting "I'll see you later" and slamming the front door, she was gone.

"Where is she off to?" said Mum.

"She's going to Alfie's" said Dad.